Northminster Nursery Sch.
7444 Buckley Road
North Syracuse, NY 13212

Library of Congress Cataloging-in-Publication Data available.

ISBN 0-590-44637-1

12 11 10 9 8 7 6 5 4 3 2 1   3 4 5 6 7 8/9

Printed in Malaysia

First Scholastic printing, January 1993

H·U·G·S

By Alice McLerran
Illustrated by Mary Morgan

SCHOLASTIC INC.
New York Toronto London Auckland Sydney

Hugs are almost magic,
Hugs are fun to do.
Other people give you hugs,
You can give hugs, too.

A hug can mean "Hello there!"

A hug can mean "Good-bye."

A hug can mean "I love you."

A hug can mean "Don't cry."

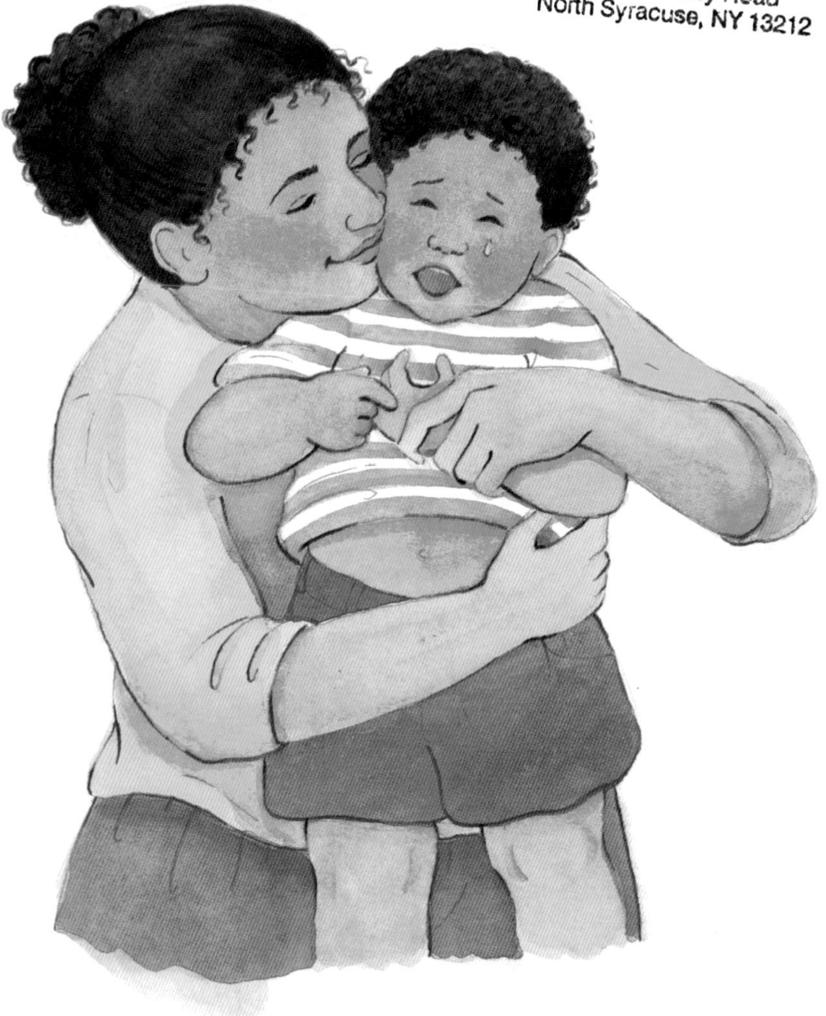

Grown-ups like to hug you,
They like it quite a lot.

At times you want to hug them back.
At times you'd rather not.

A kitten sometimes likes a hug,
But just a very light one.

Daddy always loves a hug
And it can be a tight one.

Grandma likes to send a hug
Tucked inside a letter.

If you fall and bump your knee,
A hug can make it better.

Sometimes when a thing goes wrong
A hug can make it right.

A great big hug at bedtime
Will keep you warm all night.

Hugs are almost magic.
Hugs are fun to do.

There's someone who could use a hug
Right now. Can you guess who?